The Rocking Horse Winner & Other Stories

The Rocking Horse Winner
& Other Stories
D. H. Lawrence

The Rocking Horse Winner & Other Stories by D. H. Lawrence

This edition has been published in 2018 in the
United Kingdom by Paper + Ink.

www.paperand.ink
Twitter: @paper_andink
Instagram: paper_and.ink

The stories featured in this edition first appeared in *The Woman
Who Rode Away, and Other Stories* ("The Rocking Horse Winner" and
"Smile"), published in 1928 by Martin Secker (London) and *The
Prussian Officer and Other Stories* ("A Sick Collier"), published
in 1941 by Gerald Duckworth and Company, Ltd (London).
Minor changes to punctuation, spelling and formatting have been made.

1 2 3 4 5 6 7 8 9 10

ISBN 9781911475170

A CIP catalogue record for this book is available from the British Library.

Typeset and jacket design by James Nunn: www.jamesnunn.co.uk | @Gnunkse

Printed and bound in Poland by Opolgraf: www.opolgraf.com

CONTENTS

THE ROCKING HORSE WINNER

There was a woman who was beautiful, who started with all the advantages, yet she had no luck. She married for love, and the love turned to dust. She had bonny children, yet she felt they had been thrust upon her, and she could not love them. They looked at her coldly, as if they were finding fault with her. And hurriedly, she felt she must cover up some fault in herself. Yet what it was that she must cover up, she never knew. Nevertheless, when her children were present, she always felt the centre of her heart go hard. This troubled her, and in her manner she was all the more gentle and anxious for her children, as if she loved them very much. Only she herself knew that at the centre of her heart was a hard little place that could not feel love, no, not for anybody. Everybody else said of her: "She is such a good mother. She adores her children." Only she herself, and her children themselves, knew it was not so. They read it in each other's eyes.

There were a boy and two little girls. They lived in a pleasant house with a garden, and they had discreet servants and felt themselves superior to anyone in the neighbourhood. Although they lived in style, they felt always an anxiety in the house. There was never enough money. The mother had a small income, and the father had a small income, but not nearly enough for the social position that they had to keep up. The father went into town to some office. But though he had good prospects, these prospects never materialised. There was always a grinding sense of the shortage of money, though the style was always kept up.

At last, the mother said: "I will see if I can't make something." But she did not know where to begin. She racked her brains, and tried this thing and the other, but could not find anything successful. The failure made deep lines come into her face. Her children were growing up; they would have to go to school. There must be more money, there must be more money. The father, who was always very handsome and expensive in his tastes, seemed as if he never would be able to do anything worth doing. And the mother, who had a great belief in herself, did not succeed any better, and her tastes were just as expensive.

And so the house came to be haunted by the unspoken phrase: *There must be more money!*

There must be more money! The children could hear it all the time, though nobody said it aloud. They heard it at Christmas, when the expensive and splendid toys filled the nursery. Behind the shining, modern rocking horse, behind the smart doll's house, a voice would start whispering: *There must be more money! There must be more money!* And the children would stop playing, to listen for a moment. They would look into each other's eyes, to see if they had all heard. And each one saw in the eyes of the other two that they, too, had heard. *There must be more money! There must be more money!*

It came whispering from the springs of the still-swaying rocking horse, and even the horse, bending his wooden, champing head, heard it. The big doll, sitting so pink and smirking in her new pram, could hear it quite plainly, and seemed to be smirking all the more self-consciously because of it. The foolish puppy, too, that took the place of the teddy bear, was looking so extraordinarily foolish for no other reason but that he heard the secret whisper all over the house: *There must be more money!* Yet nobody ever said it aloud. The whisper was everywhere, and therefore no one spoke it. Just as no one ever says: "We are breathing!" in spite of the fact that breath is coming and going all the time.

"Mother," said the boy Paul one day, "why don't we keep a car of our own? Why do we always use uncle's, or else a taxi?"

"Because we're the poor members of the family," said the mother.

"But why are we, Mother?"

"Well ... I suppose," she said slowly and bitterly, "it's because your father has no luck."

The boy was silent for some time. "Is luck

money, Mother?" he asked, rather timidly.

"No, Paul. Not quite. It's what causes you to have money."

"Oh!" said Paul vaguely. "I thought when Uncle Oscar said 'filthy lucker', it meant money."

"'Filthy lucre' does mean money," said the mother. "But it's *lucre*, not luck."

"Oh!" said the boy. "Then what is luck, Mother?"

"It's what causes you to have money. If you're lucky, you have money. That's why it's better to be born lucky than rich. If you're rich, you may lose your money. But if you're lucky, you will always get more money."

"Oh! Will you? And is Father not lucky?"

"Very unlucky, I should say," she said bitterly.

The boy watched her with unsure eyes.

"Why?" he asked.

"I don't know. Nobody ever knows why one person is lucky and another unlucky."

"Don't they? Nobody at all? Does nobody know?"

"Perhaps God. But He never tells."

"He ought to, then. And aren't you lucky either, Mother?"

"I can't be, I married an unlucky husband."

"But by yourself, aren't you?"

"I used to think I was, before I married. Now I think I am very unlucky indeed."

"Why?"

"Well ... never mind! Perhaps I'm not, really," she said.

The child looked at her to see if she meant it. But he saw, by the lines of her mouth, that she was only trying to hide something from him.

"Well, anyhow," he said stoutly, "I'm a lucky person."

"Why?" said his mother, with a sudden laugh.

He stared at her. He didn't even know why he had said it.

"God told me," he asserted, brazening it out.

"I hope He did, dear!" she said, again with a laugh, but rather bitter.

"He did, Mother!"

"Excellent!" said the mother, using one of her husband's exclamations.

The boy saw she did not believe him; or rather, that she paid no attention to his assertion. This angered him somewhere, and made him want to compel her attention.

He went off by himself, vaguely, in a childish way, seeking for the clue to "luck". Absorbed, taking no heed of other people, he went about with a sort of stealth, seeking inwardly for luck. He wanted luck, he wanted it, he wanted it. When the two girls were playing dolls in the nursery, he would sit on his big rocking horse, charging madly into space, with a frenzy that made the little girls peer at him uneasily. Wildly the horse careered, the waving dark hair of the boy tossed; his eyes had a strange glare in them. The little girls dared not speak to him.

When he had ridden to the end of his mad little journey, he climbed down and stood in front of his rocking horse, staring fixedly into its lowered face. Its red mouth was slightly open; its big eye was wide and glassy-bright.

"Now!" he would silently command the snorting steed. "Now take me to where there is luck! Now take me!"

And he would slash the horse on the neck with the little whip he had asked Uncle Oscar for. He knew the horse could take him to where there was luck, if only he forced it. So he would mount again and start on his furious ride, hoping at last to get there.

"You'll break your horse, Paul!" said the nurse.

"He's always riding like that! I wish he'd leave off!" said his elder sister Joan.

But he only glared down on them in silence. Nurse gave him up. She could make nothing of him. Anyhow, he was growing beyond her.

One day, his mother and his Uncle Oscar came in when he was on one of his furious rides. He did not speak to them.

"Hallo, you young jockey! Riding a winner?" said his uncle.

"Aren't you growing too big for a rocking horse? You're not a very little boy any longer, you know," said his mother.

But Paul only gave a blue glare from his big, rather close-set eyes. He would speak to nobody when he was in full tilt. His mother watched him with an anxious expression on her face. At last, he suddenly stopped forcing his horse into the mechanical gallop and slid down.

"Well, I got there!" he announced fiercely, his blue eyes still flaring, and his sturdy long legs straddling apart.

"Where did you get to?" asked his mother.

"Where I wanted to go," he flared back at her.

"That's right, son!" said Uncle Oscar. "Don't you stop till you get there. What's the horse's name?"

"He doesn't have a name," said the boy.

"Gets on without all right?" asked the uncle.

"Well, he has different names. He was called 'Sansovino' last week."

"Sansovino, eh? Won the Ascot. How did you know this name?"

"He always talks about horse races with Bassett," said Joan.

The uncle was delighted to find that his small nephew was posted with all the racing news. Bassett, the young gardener, who had been wounded in the left foot in the war and had got his present job through Oscar Cresswell, whose batman he had been, was a perfect blade of the 'turf'. He lived in the racing events, and the small boy lived with him.

Oscar Cresswell got it all from Bassett.

"Master Paul comes and asks me, so I can't do more than tell him, sir," said Bassett, his face terribly serious, as if he were speaking of religious matters.

"And does he ever put anything on a horse he fancies?"

"Well – I don't want to give him away ... he's a young sport, a fine sport, sir. Would you mind asking him himself? He sort of takes a pleasure in it, and perhaps he'd feel I was giving him away, sir, if you don't mind."

Bassett was serious as a church. The uncle went back to his nephew and took him off for a ride in the car.

"Say, Paul, old man, do you ever put anything on a horse?" the uncle asked.

The boy watched the handsome man closely. "Why, do you think I oughtn't to?" he parried.

"Not a bit of it! I thought perhaps you might give me a tip for the Lincoln."

The car sped on into the country, going down to Uncle Oscar's place in Hampshire.

"Honour bright?" said the nephew.

"Honour bright, son!" said the uncle.

"Well, then ... Daffodil."

"Daffodil! I doubt it, sonny. What about Mirza?"

"I only know the winner," said the boy.

"That's Daffodil."

"Daffodil, eh?" There was a pause. Daffodil was an obscure horse, comparatively.

"Uncle!"

"Yes, son?"

"You won't let it go any further, will you? I promised Bassett."

"Bassett be damned, old man! What's he got to do with it?"

"We're partners. We've been partners from the first. Uncle, he lent me my first five shillings, which I lost. I promised him, honour bright, it was only between me and him; only you gave me that ten-shilling note I started winning with, so I thought you were lucky. You won't let it go any further, will you?"

The boy gazed at his uncle from those big, hot, blue eyes, set rather close together. The uncle stirred and laughed uneasily.

"Right you are, son! I'll keep your tip

private. How much are you putting on him?"

"All except twenty pounds," said the boy. "I keep that in reserve."

The uncle thought it a good joke.

"You keep twenty pounds in reserve, do you, you young romancer? What are you betting, then?"

"I'm betting three hundred," said the boy gravely. "But it's between you and me, Uncle Oscar! Honour bright?"

"It's between you and me all right, you young Nat Gould," he said, laughing. "But where's your three hundred?"

"Bassett keeps it for me. We're partners."

"You are, are you! And what is Bassett putting on Daffodil?"

"He won't go quite as high as I do, I expect. Perhaps he'll go a hundred and fifty."

"What, pennies?" laughed the uncle.

"Pounds," said the child, with a surprised

look at his uncle. "Bassett keeps a bigger reserve than I do."

Between wonder and amusement, Uncle Oscar was silent. He pursued the matter no further, but he determined to take his nephew with him to the Lincoln races.

"Now, son," he said, "I'm putting twenty on Mirza, and I'll put five on for you on any horse you fancy. What's your pick?"

"Daffodil, Uncle."

"No, not the fiver on Daffodil!"

"I should if it was my own fiver," said the child.

"Good! Good! Right you are! A fiver for me and a fiver for you on Daffodil."

The child had never been to a race meeting before, and his eyes were blue fire. He pursed his mouth tight, and watched. A Frenchman just in front had put his money on Lancelot. Wild with excitement, he flayed his arms up and down, yelling "Lancelot! Lancelot!" in his French accent.

Daffodil came in first, Lancelot second, Mirza third. The child, flushed and with eyes blazing, was curiously serene. His uncle brought him four five-pound notes, four to one.

"What am I to do with these?" he cried, waving them before the boy's eyes.

"I suppose we'll talk to Bassett," said the boy. "I expect I have fifteen hundred now, and twenty in reserve – and this twenty."

His uncle studied him for some moments.

"Look here, son!" he said. "You're not serious about Bassett and that fifteen hundred, are you?"

"Yes, I am. But it's between you and me, Uncle. Honour bright?"

"Honour bright all right, son! But I must talk to Bassett."

"If you'd like to be a partner, Uncle, with Bassett and me, we could all be partners. Only, you'd have to promise, honour bright, Uncle, not to let it go beyond us three. Bassett and I are lucky, and you must be lucky, because it was your ten shillings I started winning with ..."

Uncle Oscar took both Bassett and Paul into Richmond Park for an afternoon, and there they talked.

"It's like this, you see, sir," Bassett said. "Master Paul would get me talking about racing events, spinning yarns, you know, sir. And he was always keen on knowing if I'd made or if I'd lost. It's about a year since, now, that I put five shillings on Blush of Dawn for him; and we lost. Then the luck turned, with that ten shillings he had from you: that we put on Singhalese. And since that time, it's been pretty steady, all things considering. What do you say, Master Paul?"

"We're all right when we're sure," said Paul. "It's when we're not quite sure that we go down."

"Oh, but we're careful then," said Bassett.

"But when are you sure?" smiled Uncle Oscar.

"It's Master Paul, sir," said Bassett in a secret, religious voice. "It's as if he had it from Heaven. Like Daffodil, now, for the Lincoln. That was as sure as eggs."

"Did you put anything on Daffodil?" asked Oscar Cresswell.

"Yes, sir, I made my bit."

"And my nephew?"

Bassett was obstinately silent, looking at Paul.

"I made twelve hundred, didn't I, Bassett? I told uncle I was putting three hundred on Daffodil."

"That's right," said Bassett, nodding.

"But where's the money?" asked the uncle.

"I keep it safe locked up, sir. Master Paul, he can have it any minute he likes to ask for it."

"What, fifteen hundred pounds?"

"And twenty! And forty, that is, with the twenty he made on the course."

"It's amazing!" said the uncle.

"If Master Paul offers you to be partners, sir, I would, if I were you; if you'll excuse me," said Bassett.

Oscar Cresswell thought about it. "I'll see the money," he said.

They drove home again, and, sure enough, Bassett came round to the garden-house with fifteen hundred pounds in notes. The twenty pounds' reserve was left with Joe Glee, in the Turf Commission deposit.

"You see, it's all right, Uncle, when I'm sure! Then we go strong, for all we're worth, don't we, Bassett?"

"We do that, Master Paul."

"And when are you sure?" said the uncle, laughing.

"Oh, well, sometimes I'm absolutely sure, like about Daffodil," said the boy; "and sometimes I have an idea; and sometimes I haven't even an idea, have I, Bassett? Then we're careful, because we mostly go down."

"You do, do you! And when you're sure, like about Daffodil, what makes you sure, sonny?"

"Oh, well, I don't know," said the boy uneasily. "I'm sure, you know, Uncle; that's all."

"It's as if he had it from Heaven, sir," Bassett reiterated.

"I should say so!" said the uncle. But he became a partner. And when the Leger was coming on, Paul was "sure" about Lively Spark, which was a quite inconsiderable horse. The boy insisted on putting a thousand on the horse; Bassett went for five hundred; and Oscar Cresswell, two hundred. Lively Spark came in first, and the betting had been ten to one against him. Paul had made ten thousand.

"You see," he said. "I was absolutely sure of him."

Even Oscar Cresswell had cleared two thousand. "Look here, son," he said, "this sort of thing makes me nervous."

"It needn't, Uncle! Perhaps I shan't be sure again for a long time."

"But what are you going to do with your money?" asked the uncle.

"Of course," said the boy, "I started it for Mother. She said she had no luck, because father is unlucky, so I thought if I was lucky, it might stop whispering."

"What might stop whispering?"

"Our house. I hate our house for

whispering."

"What does it whisper?"

"Why ... why ..." – the boy fidgeted – "why, I don't know. But it's always short of money, you know, Uncle."

"I know it, son, I know it."

"You know people send mother writs, don't you, Uncle?"

"I'm afraid I do," said the uncle.

"And then the house whispers, like people laughing at you behind your back. It's awful, that is! I thought if I was lucky –"

"You might stop it," added the uncle.

The boy watched him with big blue eyes that had an uncanny, cold fire in them, and he said never a word.

"Well, then!" said the uncle. "What are we doing?"

"I shouldn't like Mother to know I was lucky," said the boy.

"Why not, son?"

"She'd stop me."

"I don't think she would."

"Oh!" – and the boy writhed in an odd way – "I don't want her to know, Uncle."

"All right, son! We'll manage it without her knowing."

They managed it very easily. Paul, at the other's suggestion, handed over five thousand pounds to his uncle, who deposited it with the family lawyer, who was then to inform Paul's mother that a relative had put five thousand pounds into his hands, which sum was to be paid out a thousand pounds at a time, on the mother's birthday, for the next five years. "So she'll have a birthday present of a thousand pounds for five successive years," said Uncle Oscar. "I hope it won't make it all the harder for her later."

Paul's mother had her birthday in

November. The house had been "whispering" worse than ever lately, and even in spite of his luck, Paul could not bear up against it. He was very anxious to see the effect of the birthday letter, telling his mother about the thousand pounds.

When there were no visitors, Paul now took his meals with his parents, as he was beyond the nursery's control. His mother went into town nearly every day. She had discovered that she had an odd knack of sketching furs and dress materials, so she worked secretly in the studio of a friend who was the chief "artist" for the leading drapers. She drew the figures of ladies in furs and ladies in silk and sequins for the newspaper advertisements. This young woman artist earned several thousand pounds a year, but Paul's mother only made several hundred, and she was again dissatisfied. She so wanted to be first in something, and she did not succeed, even in making sketches for drapery advertisements.

She was down to breakfast on the morning of her birthday. Paul watched her face as she read her letters. He knew the lawyer's letter. As his mother read it, her face hardened and became more expressionless. Then a cold, determined look came on her mouth. She hid the letter under the pile of others, and said not a word about it.

"Didn't you have anything nice in the post for your birthday, Mother?" said Paul.

"Quite moderately nice," she said, her voice cold and hard and absent. She went away to town without saying more.

But in the afternoon, Uncle Oscar appeared. He said Paul's mother had had a long interview with the lawyer, asking if the whole five thousand could not be advanced at once, as she was in debt.

"What do you think, Uncle?" said the boy.

"I leave it to you, son."

"Oh, let her have it, then! We can get some more with the other," said the boy.

"A bird in the hand is worth two in the bush, laddie!" said Uncle Oscar.

"But I'm sure to know for the Grand National, or the Lincolnshire, or else the Derby. I'm sure to know for one of them," said Paul.

So Uncle Oscar signed the agreement, and Paul's mother touched the whole five thousand. Then something very curious happened. The voices in the house suddenly went mad, like a chorus of frogs on a spring evening. There were certain new furnishings, and Paul had a tutor. He was really going to Eton, his father's school, the following autumn. There were flowers in the winter, and a blossoming of the luxury Paul's mother had been used to. And yet the voices in the house, behind the sprays of mimosa and almond-blossom, and from under the piles of iridescent cushions, simply trilled and screamed in a sort of ecstasy: *There must be more money! Ohhh, there must be more money. Oh, now, noww! Nowww – there must be more money! More than ever! More than ever!*

It frightened Paul terribly. He studied away at his Latin and Greek with his tutor. But his intense hours were spent with Bassett. The Grand National had gone by: he had not "known", and had lost a hundred pounds. Summer was at hand. He was in agony for the Lincoln. But even for the Lincoln he didn't "know", and he lost fifty pounds. He became wild-eyed and strange, as if something were going to explode in him.

"Let it alone, son! Don't you bother about it!" urged Uncle Oscar. But it was as if the boy couldn't really hear what his uncle was saying.

"I've got to know for the Derby! I've got to know for the Derby!" the child reiterated, his big blue eyes blazing with a sort of madness.

His mother noticed how overwrought he was.

"You'd better go to the seaside. Wouldn't you like to go now to the seaside, instead of waiting? I think you'd better," she said, looking down at him anxiously, her heart curiously heavy because of him.

But the child lifted his uncanny blue eyes. "I couldn't possibly go before the Derby, Mother!" he said. "I couldn't possibly!"

"Why not?" she said, her voice becoming heavy when she was opposed. "Why not? You can still go from the seaside to see the Derby with your Uncle Oscar, if that's what you wish. No need for you to wait here. Besides, I think you care too much about these races. It's a bad sign. My family has been a gambling family, and you won't know till you grow up how much damage it has done. But it has done damage. I shall have to send Bassett away, and ask Uncle Oscar not to talk racing to you, unless you promise to be reasonable about it: go away to the seaside and forget it. You're all nerves!"

"I'll do what you like, Mother, so long as you don't send me away till after the Derby," the boy said.

"Send you away from where? Just from this house?"

"Yes," he said, gazing at her.

"Why, you curious child, what makes you care about this house so much, suddenly? I never knew you loved it."

He gazed at her without speaking. He had a secret within a secret, something he had not divulged, even to Bassett or to his

Uncle Oscar.

But his mother, after standing undecided and a little bit sullen for some moments, said: "Very well, then! Don't go to the seaside till after the Derby, if you don't wish it. But promise me you won't think so much about horse racing and events, as you call them!"

"Oh no," said the boy casually. "I won't think much about them, Mother. You needn't worry. I wouldn't worry, Mother, if I were you."

"If you were me and I were you," said his mother, "I wonder what we should do!"

"But you know you needn't worry, Mother, don't you?" the boy repeated.

"I should be awfully glad to know it," she said wearily.

"Oh, well, you can, you know. I mean, you ought to know you needn't worry," he insisted.

"Ought I? Then I'll see about it," she said.

Paul's secret of secrets was his wooden

horse, which had no name. Since he was emancipated from a nurse and a nursery governess, he had had his rocking horse removed to his own bedroom at the top of the house.

"Surely you're too big for a rocking horse!" his mother had remonstrated.

"Well, you see, Mother, till I can have a real horse, I like to have some sort of animal about," had been his quaint answer.

"Do you feel he keeps you company?" she laughed.

"Oh, yes! He's very good; he always keeps me company when I'm there," said Paul.

So the horse, rather shabby, stood in an arrested prance in the boy's bedroom.

The Derby was drawing near, and the boy grew more and more tense. He hardly heard what was spoken to him; he was very frail, and his eyes were uncanny. His mother had sudden strange seizures of uneasiness about him. Sometimes, for half an hour, she would feel an anxiety about him that was almost anguish. She wanted to rush to him at once, and know he was safe.

Two nights before the Derby, she was at a big party in town when one of her rushes of anxiety about her boy, her first-born, gripped her heart till she could hardly speak. She fought with the feeling, might and main, for she believed in common sense. But it was too strong. She had to leave the dance and go downstairs to telephone to the country. The children's nursery governess was terribly surprised and startled at being rung up in the night.

"Are the children all right, Miss Wilmot?"

"Oh yes, they are quite all right."

"Master Paul? Is he all right?"

"He went to bed as right as a trivet. Shall I run up and look at him?"

"No," said Paul's mother reluctantly. "No! Don't trouble. It's all right. Don't sit up. We shall be home fairly soon." She did not want her son's privacy intruded upon.

"Very good," said the governess.

It was about one o'clock when Paul's mother and father drove up to their house. All was still. Paul's mother went to her room and slipped off her white fur cloak. She had told her maid not to wait up for her. She heard her husband downstairs, mixing a whisky and soda.

And then, because of the strange anxiety at her heart, she stole upstairs to her son's room. Noiselessly, she went along the upper corridor. Was there a faint noise? What was it?

She stood, with arrested muscles, outside his door, listening. There was a strange, heavy and yet not loud noise. Her heart stood still. It was a soundless noise, yet rushing and powerful. Something huge, in violent, hushed motion. What was it? What in God's name was it? She ought to know. She felt that she knew the noise. She knew what it was. Yet she could not place it. She couldn't say what it was. And on and on it went, like a madness.

Softly, frozen with anxiety and fear, she turned the door handle.

The room was dark. Yet in the space near the window, she heard and saw something plunging to and fro. She gazed in fear and amazement.

Then, suddenly, she switched on the light and saw her son, in his green pyjamas, madly surging on the rocking horse. The blaze of light suddenly lit him up, as he urged the wooden horse, and lit her up, as she stood, blonde, in her dress of pale green and crystal, in the doorway.

"Paul!" she cried. "Whatever are you doing?"

41

"It's Malabar!" he screamed in a powerful, strange voice. "It's Malabar!"

His eyes blazed at her for one strange and senseless second, as he ceased urging his wooden horse. Then he fell with a crash to the ground, and she, all her tormented motherhood flooding upon her, rushed to gather him up.

But he was unconscious, and unconscious he remained, with some brain-fever. He talked and tossed, and his mother sat stonily by his side.

"Malabar! It's Malabar! Bassett, Bassett, I know! It's Malabar!"

So the child cried, trying to get up and urge the rocking horse that gave him his inspiration.

"What does he mean by 'Malabar'?" asked the heart-frozen mother.

"I don't know," said the father stonily.

"What does he mean by 'Malabar'?" she

asked her brother Oscar.

"It's one of the horses running for the Derby," was the answer.

And, in spite of himself, Oscar Cresswell spoke to Bassett, and himself put a thousand on Malabar: at fourteen to one.

The third day of the illness was critical: they were waiting for a change. The boy, with his rather long, curly hair, was tossing ceaselessly on the pillow. He neither slept nor regained consciousness, and his eyes were like blue stones. His mother sat, feeling her heart had gone, turned actually into a stone.

In the evening, Oscar Cresswell did not come, but Bassett sent a message, saying could he come up for one moment, just one moment? Paul's mother was very angry at the intrusion, but on second thought she agreed. The boy was the same. Perhaps Bassett might bring him to consciousness.

The gardener, a shortish fellow with a little brown moustache and sharp, little brown eyes, tiptoed into the room, touched his imaginary cap to Paul's mother and stole to the bedside, staring with glittering, smallish eyes at the tossing, dying child.

"Master Paul!" he whispered. "Master Paul! Malabar came in first, all right, a clean win. I did as you told me. You've made over seventy thousand pounds, you have; you've got over *eighty* thousand. Malabar came in all right, Master Paul."

"Malabar! Malabar! Did I say Malabar, Mother? Did I say Malabar? Do you think I'm lucky, Mother? I knew 'Malabar', didn't I? Over eighty thousand pounds! I call that lucky, don't you, Mother? Over eighty thousand pounds! I knew, didn't I know I knew? Malabar came in all right. If I ride my horse till I'm sure, then I tell you, Bassett, you can go as high as you like. Did you go for all you were worth, Bassett?"

"I went a thousand on it, Master Paul."

"I never told you, Mother, that if I can ride my horse, and get there, then I'm absolutely sure – oh, absolutely! Mother, did I ever tell you? I am lucky!"

"No, you never did," said his mother.

But the boy died in the night.

And even as he lay dead, his mother heard her brother's voice saying to her: "My God, Hester, you're eighty-odd thousand to the good, and a poor devil of a son to the bad. But poor devil, poor devil, he's best gone out of a life where he rides his rocking horse to find a winner."

A SICK
COLLIER

She was too good for him, everybody said.
Yet still she did not regret marrying him.
He had come courting her when he was only
nineteen, and she twenty. He was, in build,
what they call a tight, little fellow: short,
dark, with a warm colour, and that upright
set of the head and chest, that flaunting way
in movement recalling a mating bird, which
denotes a body taut and compact with life.
Being a good worker, he had earned decent
money in the mine, and, having a good home,
had saved a little.

She was a cook at Uplands, a tall, fair girl,

very quiet. Having seen her walk down the street, Horsepool had followed her from a distance. He was taken with her. He did not drink, and he was not lazy. So, although he seemed a bit simple, without much intelligence but having a sort of physical brightness, she considered, and accepted him.

When they were married, they went to live in Scargill Street, in a highly respectable six-roomed house that they had furnished between them. The street was built up the side of a long, steep hill. It was narrow and rather tunnel-like. Nevertheless, the back looked out over the adjoining pasture, across a wide valley of fields and woods, at the bottom of which the mine lay snugly.

He made himself gaffer in his own house. She was unacquainted with a collier's mode of life. They were married on a Saturday. On the Sunday night he said: "Set th' table for my breakfast, an' put my pit-things afront o' th' fire. I's'll be gettin' up at ha'ef pas' five. Tha nedna shift thysen, not till when ter likes." He showed her how to put a newspaper on the table for a cloth. When she demurred: "I want none o' your white cloths i' th' mornin'. I like ter be able to slobber if I feel like it," he said.

He put before the fire his moleskin trousers, a clean singlet, or sleeveless vest of thick flannel, a pair of stockings and his pit boots, arranging them all to be warm and ready for morning.

"Now tha sees. That wants doin' ivery night."

Punctually, at half past five, he left her, without any form of leave-taking, going downstairs in his shirt. When he arrived home at four o'clock in the afternoon, his dinner was ready to be dished up. She was startled when he came in, a short, sturdy figure with a face indescribably black and streaked. She stood before the fire in her white blouse and white apron, a fair girl, the picture of beautiful cleanliness. He "clommaxed" in, in his heavy boots.

"Well, how 'as ter gone on?" he asked.

"I was ready for you to come home," she replied tenderly. In his black face, the whites of his brown eyes flashed at her.

"An' I wor ready for comin'," he said. He planked his tin bottle and snap-bag on the dresser, took off his coat and scarf and waistcoat, dragged his armchair nearer the fire and sat down.

"Let's ha'e a bit o' dinner, then – I'm about clammed," he said.

"Aren't you goin' to wash yourself first?"

"What am I to wesh mysen for?"

"Well, you can't eat your dinner –"

"Oh, strike a daisy, Missis! Dunna I eat my

snap i' th' pit wi'out weshin'? Forced to."

She served the dinner and sat opposite him. His small bullet head was quite black, save for the whites of his eyes and his scarlet lips. It gave her a queer sensation to see him open his red mouth and bare his white teeth as he ate. His arms and hands were mottled black; his bare, strong neck got a little fairer as it settled towards his shoulders, reassuring her. There was the faint, indescribable odour of the pit in the room, an odour of damp, exhausted air.

"Why is your vest so black on the shoulders?" she asked.

"My singlet? That's wi' th' watter droppin' on us from th' roof. This is a dry 'un as I put on afore I come up. They ha'e gre't clothes-'osses, an' as we change us things, we put 'em on theer ter dry."

When he washed himself, kneeling on

the hearth-rug stripped to the waist, she felt afraid of him again. He was so muscular; he seemed so intent on what he was doing, so intensely himself, like a vigorous animal. And as he stood wiping himself, with his naked breast towards her, she felt rather sick, seeing his thick arms bulge their muscles.

They were nevertheless very happy. He was at a great pitch of pride because of her. The men in the pit might chaff him, they might try to entice him away, but nothing could reduce his self-assured pride because of her, nothing could unsettle his almost infantile satisfaction. In the evening he sat in his armchair chattering to her, or listening as she read the newspaper to him. When it was fine, he would go into the street, squat on his heels as colliers do, with his back against the wall of his parlour, and call to the passers-by in greeting, one after another. If no one were passing, he was content just to squat and smoke, having such a fund of sufficiency and satisfaction in his heart. He was well married.

They had not been wed a year when all Brent and Wellwood's men came out on strike. Willy was in the Union, so with a pinch they scrambled through. The furniture was not all paid for, and other debts were incurred. She worried and contrived; he left it to her. But he was a good husband. He gave her all he had.

The men were out fifteen weeks. They had been back just over a year when Willy had an accident in the mine, tearing his bladder. At the pit head, the doctor talked of the hospital. Losing his head entirely, the young collier raved like a madman, what with pain and fear of hospital. "Tha s'lt go whoam, Willy, tha s'lt go whoam," the deputy said.

A lad warned the wife to have the bed ready. Without speaking or hesitating, she prepared. But when the ambulance came, and she heard him shout with pain at being moved, she was afraid lest she should sink down. They carried him in.

"Yo' should 'a' had a bed i' th' parlour, Missis," said the deputy, "then we shouldna ha' had to hawkse 'im upstairs, an' it 'ud 'a' saved your legs." But it was too late now. They got him upstairs.

"They let me lie, Lucy," he was crying, "they let me lie two mortal hours on th' sleck afore they took me outer th' stall. Th' peen, Lucy, th' peen; oh, Lucy, th' peen, th' peen!"

"I know th' pain's bad, Willy, I know. But you must try an' bear it a bit."

"Tha munna carry on in that form, lad, thy missis'll niver be able ter stan' it," said the deputy.

"I canna 'elp it, it's th' peen, it's th' peen," he cried again. He had never been ill in his life.

When he had smashed a finger he could look at the wound. But this pain came from inside, and terrified him. At last, he was soothed and exhausted.

It was some time before she could undress him and wash him. He would let no other woman do for him, having that savage modesty usual in such men.

For six weeks he was in bed, suffering much pain. The doctors were not quite sure what was the matter with him, and scarcely knew what to do. He could eat; he did not lose flesh, nor strength; yet the pain continued, and he could hardly walk at all.

In the sixth week, the men came out in the national strike. He would get up quite early in the morning and sit by the window. On Wednesday, the second week of the strike, he sat gazing out on the street as usual, a bullet-headed young man, still vigorous-looking, but with a peculiar expression of hunted fear in his face.

"Lucy," he called, "Lucy!"

She, pale and worn, ran upstairs at his bidding.

"Gi'e me a han'kercher," he said.

"Why, you've got one," she replied, coming near.

"Tha nedna touch me," he cried. Feeling his pocket, he produced a white handkerchief.

"I non want a white un, gi'e me a red un," he said.

"An' if anybody comes to see you," she answered, giving him a red handkerchief. "Besides," she continued, "you needn't ha' brought me upstairs for that."

"I b'lieve th' peen's commin' on again," he said, with a little horror in his voice.

"It isn't, you know, it isn't," she replied. "The doctor says you imagine it's there when it isn't."

"Canna I feel what's inside me?" he shouted.

"There's a traction-engine coming downhill," she said. "That'll scatter them. I'll just go an' finish your pudding."

She left him. The traction-engine went by, shaking the houses. Then the street was quiet, save for the men. A gang of youths from fifteen to twenty-five years old were playing marbles in the middle of the road. Other little groups of men were playing on the pavement. The street was gloomy. Willy could hear the endless calling and shouting of men's voices.

"Tha'rt skinchin'!"

"I arena!"

"Come 'ere with that blood-alley."

"Swop us four for't."

"Shonna, gie's hold on't."

He wanted to be out, he wanted to be playing marbles. The pain had weakened his mind so that he hardly knew any self-control.

Presently another gang of men lounged up the street. It was pay morning. The Union was paying the men in the Primitive Chapel. They were returning with their half-sovereigns.

"Sorry!" bawled a voice. "Sorry!" The word is a form of address, a corruption probably of "Sirrah". Willy started almost out of his chair. "Sorry!" again bawled a great voice. "Art goin' wi' me to see Notts play Villa?"

Many of the marble players started up. "What time is it? There's no treens, we s'll ha'e ter walk." The street was alive with men.

"Who's goin' ter Nottingham ter see th' match?" shouted the same big voice. A very large, tipsy man, with his cap over his eyes, was calling.

"Com' on – aye, com' on!" came many voices. The street was full of the shouting of men. They split up in excited cliques and groups.

"Play up, Notts!" the big man shouted.

"Plee up, Notts!" shouted the youths and men. They were at kindling pitch. It only needed a shout to rouse them. Of this, the careful authorities were aware.

"I'm goin', I'm goin'!" shouted the sick man at his window. Lucy came running upstairs. "I'm goin' ter see Notts play Villa on th' Meadows ground," he declared.

"You – you can't go. There are no trains. You can't walk nine miles."

"I'm goin' ter see th' match," he declared, rising.

"You know you can't. Sit down now an' be quiet." She put her hand on him. He shook it off.

"Leave me alone, leave me alone. It's thee as ma'es th' peen come, it's thee. I'm goin' ter Nottingham to see th' football match."

"Sit down – folks'll hear you, and what will

they think?"

"Come off'n me. Com' off. It's 'er, it's 'er as does it. Com' off."

He seized hold of her. His little head was bristling with madness, and he was strong as a lion.

"Oh, Willy!" she cried.

"It's 'er, it's 'er. Kill 'er!" he shouted. "Kill 'er!"

"Willy, folks'll hear you."

"Th' peen's commin' on again, I tell yer. I'll kill 'er for it."

He was completely out of his mind. She struggled with him to prevent his going to the stairs. When she escaped from him, he was shouting and raving. She beckoned to her neighbour, a girl of twenty-four, who was cleaning the window across the road. Ethel Mellor was the daughter of a well-to-do check-weighman. She ran across in fear to Mrs Horsepool. Hearing the man raving, people were running out in the street and listening. Ethel hurried upstairs. Everything was clean and pretty in the young home.

Willy was staggering round the room, after the slowly retreating Lucy, shouting: "Kill 'er! Kill 'er!"

"Mr Horsepool!" cried Ethel, leaning against the bed, white as the sheets, and trembling. "Whatever are you saying?"

"I tell yer it's 'er fault as th' peen comes on – I tell yer it is! Kill 'er – kill 'er!"

"Kill Mrs Horsepool!" cried the trembling girl. "Why, you're ever so fond of her, you know you are."

"The peen – I ha'e such a lot o' peen – I want to kill 'er."

He was subsiding. When he sat down, his wife collapsed in a chair, weeping noiselessly. The tears ran down Ethel's face. He sat staring out of the window; then the old, hurt look came on his face.

"What 'ave I been sayin'?" he asked, looking piteously at his wife.

"Why!" said Ethel, "you've been carrying on something awful, saying, 'Kill her, kill her!'"

"Have I, Lucy?" he faltered.

"You didn't know what you was saying," said his young wife, gently but coldly.

His face puckered up. He bit his lip, then broke into tears, sobbing uncontrollably, with his face to the window.

There was no sound in the room but of three people crying bitterly, breath caught in sobs. Suddenly Lucy put away her tears and went over to him.

"You didn't know what you was sayin', Willy, I know you didn't. I knew you didn't, all the time. It doesn't matter, Willy. Only don't do it again."

In a little while, when they were calmer, she

went downstairs with Ethel. "See if anybody is looking in the street," she said. Ethel went into the parlour and peeped through the curtains.

"Aye!" she said. "You may back your life Lena an' Mrs Severn'll be out gorping, and that clat-fartin' Mrs Allsop."

"Oh, I hope they haven't heard anything! If it gets about as he's out of his mind, they'll stop his compensation, I know they will."

"They'd never stop his compensation for that," protested Ethel.

"Well, they have been stopping some –"

"It'll not get about. I's'll tell nobody."

"Oh, but if it does, whatever shall we do ...?"

SMILE

He had decided to sit up all night, as a kind of penance. The telegram had simply said: OPHELIA'S CONDITION CRITICAL. He felt, under the circumstances, that to go to bed in the wagon-lit would be frivolous. So he sat wearily in the first-class compartment as night fell over France.

He ought, of course, to be sitting by Ophelia's bedside. But Ophelia didn't want him. So he sat up in the train.

Deep inside him was a black and ponderous weight: like some tumour filled with sheer gloom, weighing down his vitals. He had always taken life seriously. Seriousness now overwhelmed him. His dark, handsome, clean-shaven face would have done for Christ on the Cross, with the thick black eyebrows tilted in the dazed agony.

The night in the train was like an inferno: nothing was real. Two elderly Englishwomen opposite him had died long ago, perhaps even before he had. Because, of course, he was dead himself.

Slow, grey dawn came in the mountains of the frontier, and he watched it with unseeing eyes. But his mind repeated:

And when the dawn came, dim and sad
And chill with early showers,
Her quiet eyelids closed: she had
Another morn than ours.

And his monk's changeless, tormented face showed no trace of the contempt he felt, even self-contempt, for this bathos, as his critical mind judged it.

He was in Italy: he looked at the country with faint aversion. Not capable of much feeling any more, he had only a tinge of aversion as he saw the olives and the sea. A sort of poetic swindle.

It was night again when he reached the home of the Blue Sisters, where Ophelia had chosen to retreat. He was ushered into the Mother Superior's room, in the palace. She rose and bowed to him in silence, looking at him along her nose. Then she said, in French: "It pains me to tell you. She died this afternoon."

He stood stupefied, not feeling much anyhow, but gazing at nothingness from his handsome, strong-featured monk's face.

The Mother Superior softly put her white, handsome hand on his arm and gazed up into his face, leaning to him. "Courage!" she said softly. "Courage, no?"

He stepped back. He was always scared when a woman leaned at him like that. In her voluminous skirts, the Mother Superior was very womanly.

"Quite!" he replied in English. "Can I see her?"

The Mother Superior rang a bell, and a young sister appeared. She was rather pale, but there was something naïve and mischievous in her hazel eyes. The elder woman murmured an introduction; the young woman demurely made a slight reverence. But Matthew held out his hand, like a man reaching for the last straw. The young nun unfolded her white hands and shyly slid one into his, passive as a sleeping bird. And out of the fathomless Hades of his gloom he thought: "What a nice hand!"

They went along a handsome but cold corridor, and tapped at a door. Matthew, walking in far-off Hades, still was aware of the soft, fine voluminousness of the women's black skirts, moving with soft, fluttered haste in front of him.

He was terrified when the door opened, and he saw the candles burning round the white bed in the lofty, noble room. A sister sat beside the candles, her face dark and primitive in the white coif as she looked up from her breviary. Then she rose, a sturdy woman, and made a little bow, and Matthew was aware of creamy-dusky hands twisting a black rosary against the rich, blue silk of her bosom.

The three sisters flocked, silent yet fluttered and very feminine in their volumes of silky black skirts, to the bedhead. The Mother Superior leaned, and with utmost delicacy lifted the veil of white lawn from the dead face.

Matthew saw the dead, beautiful composure of his wife's face, and instantly, something leaped like laughter in the depths of him; he gave a little grunt, and an extraordinary smile came over his face.

The three nuns, in the candle-glow that quivered warm and quick like a Christmas tree, were looking at him with heavily compassionate eyes from under their coif-bands. They were like a mirror. Six eyes suddenly started with a little fear, then changed, puzzled, into wonder. And over the three nuns' faces, helplessly facing him in the candle-glow, a strange, involuntary smile began to come. In the three faces, the same smile growing so differently, like three subtle flowers opening. In the pale young nun, it was almost pain, with a touch of mischievous ecstasy. But the dark Ligurian face of the watching sister, a mature, level-browed woman, curled with a pagan smile, slow, infinitely subtle in its archaic humour. It was the Etruscan smile, subtle and unabashed, and unanswerable.

The Mother Superior, who had a large-featured face something like Matthew's own, tried hard not to smile. But he kept his humorous, malevolent chin uplifted at her, and she lowered her face as the smile grew, grew and grew over her face.

The young, pale sister suddenly covered her face with her sleeve, her body shaking. The Mother Superior put her arm over the girl's shoulder, murmuring with Italian emotion: "Poor little thing! Weep, then, poor little thing!" But the chuckle was still there, under the emotion. The sturdy, dark sister stood unchanging, clutching the black beads, but the noiseless smile immovable.

Matthew suddenly turned to the bed, to see if his dead wife had observed him. It was a movement of fear.

Ophelia lay so pretty and so touching, with her peaked, dead little nose sticking up, and her face of an obstinate child fixed in the final obstinacy. The smile went away from Matthew, and the look of super-martyrdom took its place. He did not weep; he just gazed without meaning. Only, on his face deepened the look: *I knew this martyrdom was in store for me!*

She was so pretty, so childlike, so clever, so obstinate, so worn – and so dead! He felt so blank about it all.

They had been married ten years. He himself had not been perfect – no, no, not by any means! But Ophelia had always wanted her own will. She had loved him, and grown obstinate, and left him, and grown wistful, or contemptuous, or angry, a dozen times, and a dozen times come back to him.

They had no children. And he, sentimentally, had always wanted children. He felt very largely sad. Now she would never come back to him. This was the thirteenth time, and she was gone forever.

But was she? Even as he thought it, he felt her nudging him somewhere in the ribs to make him smile. He writhed a little, and an angry frown came on his brow. He was not going to smile! He set his square, naked jaw and bared his big teeth as he looked down at the infinitely provoking dead woman. *"At it again!"* he wanted to say to her, like the man in Dickens.

He himself had not been perfect. He was going to dwell on his own imperfections.

He turned suddenly to the three women,

who had faded backwards beyond the candles and now hovered, in the white frames of their coifs, between him and nowhere. His eyes glared and he bared his teeth.

"*Mea culpa! Mea culpa!*" he snarled.

"*Macché!*" exclaimed the daunted Mother Superior, and her two hands flew apart, then together again, in the density of the sleeves, like birds nesting in couples.

Matthew ducked his head and peered round, prepared to bolt. The Mother Superior, in the background, softly intoned a *Pater Noster*, and her beads dangled. The pale, young sister faded farther back. But the black eyes of the sturdy, blackavised sister twinkled like eternally humorous stars upon him, and he felt the smile digging him in the ribs again.

"Look here!" he said to the women, in

expostulation, "I'm awfully upset. I'd better go."

They hovered in fascinating bewilderment. He ducked for the door. But even as he went, the smile began to come on his face, caught by the tail of the sturdy sister's black eye, with its everlasting twinkle. And, he was secretly thinking, he wished he could hold both her creamy-dusky hands, which were folded like mating birds, voluptuously.

But he insisted on dwelling upon his own imperfections. *Mea culpa!* he howled at himself. And even as he howled it, he felt something nudge him in the ribs, saying to him: *Smile!*

The three women left behind in the lofty room looked at one another, and their hands flew up for a moment, like six birds flying suddenly out of the foliage, then settling again.

"Poor thing!" said the Mother Superior, compassionately.

"Yes! Yes! Poor thing!" cried the young sister, with naïve, shrill impulsiveness.

"*Già!*" said the darkavised sister.

The Mother Superior noiselessly moved to the bed, and leaned over the dead face.

"She seems to know, poor soul!" she murmured. "Don't you think so?"

The three coifed heads leaned together. And for the first time, they saw the faint, ironical curl at the corners of Ophelia's mouth. They looked in fluttering wonder.

"She has seen him!" whispered the thrilling young sister.

The Mother Superior delicately laid the fine-worked veil over the cold face. Then they murmured a prayer for the *anima*, fingering their beads. Then the Mother Superior set two of the candles straight upon their spikes, clenching the thick candle with a firm, soft grip and pressing it down.

The dark-faced, sturdy sister sat down again with her little holy book. The other two rustled softly to the door, and out into the great white corridor. There, softly, noiselessly sailing in all their dark drapery like dark swans down a river, they suddenly hesitated. Together they had seen a forlorn man's figure, in a melancholy overcoat, loitering in the cold distance at the corridor's end. The Mother Superior suddenly pressed her pace into an appearance of speed.

Matthew saw them bearing down on him, these voluminous figures with framed faces and lost hands. The young sister trailed a little behind.

"Pardon, ma Mère!" he said, as if in the street. "I left my hat somewhere ..."

He made a desperate, moving sweep with his arm, and never was man more utterly smileless.

NEW TITLES FROM PAPER + INK

O. Henry
The Gift of the Magi & Other Stories

Guy de Maupassant
The Necklace & Other Stories

Oscar Wilde
The Happy Prince & Other Stories

Katherine Mansfield
The Garden Party & Other Stories

Mark Twain
*The Celebrated Jumping Frog of Calaveras County
& Other Stories*

Visit **www.paperand.ink** to subscribe and receive the other books
by post, as well as to keep up to date about new volumes in the series.